SAM

THERE ARE ALWAYS TWO SIDES TO EVERY STORY.

TITLES IN TWO SIDES:

GIRL NEXT DOOR

Karen Moncrieffe

SAM

Emma Norry

YOU DON'T CARE

Luisa Plaja

STOP

Jenni Spangler

LOOKING AFTER MUM

Roy Apps

BRUISED

Donna David

Badger Publishing Limited, Oldmedow Road, Hardwick Industrial Estate, King's Lynn PE30 4JJ

Telephone: 01438 791037

www.badgerlearning.co.uk

EMMA NORRY

Sam ISBN 978-1-78837-322-7

Publisher: Susan Ross
Senior Editor: Danny Pearson
Editorial Coordinator: Claire Morgan
Copyeditor: Cheryl Lanyon
Designer: Bigtop Design Ltd
Cover Illustration: Dave Robbins

4 6 8 10 9 7 5

CHAPTER 1
STEP UP

Sam

Thank god it's Friday! Just two lessons left; I'm so over this week. Football has ended, so I sprint across the playing field towards the changing rooms. I want to get there first and, luckily, I'm a fast runner.

I skip the showers. They make me uncomfortable, everyone staring and making rude jokes about each other. I prefer to shower at home.

I take my shorts off and put my trousers on. Opening my locker, I grab my school bag, lay out my school shirt ready, and try to wiggle out of my PE T-shirt without showing too much skin.

Mason and Pranav rush in, muddy and loud, and the door bangs. "Trying to get all the hot water first, eh?" Mason yells. He puts on a silly high voice and squeals, "You getting ready for a hot date?"

Here come the insults. Can't I just be left in peace? I don't look up.

"Oi! Gay boy!" Pranav laughs. He marches over in just his boxers and slams into my shoulder, hard. Then, to Mason, "Nah, he's not even taking a shower. He wants to smell like a skank and look like one too!" He flings his dirty T-shirt at Mason's head.

I hold my T-shirt against my chest, but Mason yanks my ponytail and grabs the T-shirt out of my hands.

Now I'm bare-chested. I wrap my arms around myself, shivering, and look away. I have to bite my lip to stop my tears.

"You should lift some weights," Mason says. "Don't gays prefer it if you're butch?"

Pranav flips through the pages of the exercise book poking out of my bag. "Ooh! Who's Samantha?" he sneers.

"No one! Give it back!"

He throws it over his head to Mason. It lands on the floor and Mason drags his muddy football boot across it. "Got yourself a girlfriend, have you?"

Pranav mocks, "who would go out with this little freak?"

When Pranav was new, he got teased for being Muslim, but now it's like he doesn't even remember we used to be friends. He's choosing not to remember because if I'm being teased then everyone else will leave him alone.

Thankfully, Mr Morris walks in. He looks at

Mason and Pranav and bellows, "You jokers, get showered!"

They mumble excuses, grab their towels and rush round the corner towards the shower area.

Mr Morris is the athletics coach and my favourite teacher. He bends down and picks up my T-shirt. "You drop this?"

I nod. He throws it to me. I stuff it in my bag, turn my back and put on my school shirt, buttoning it quickly.

"Are you coming to training after class?" He hands me my exercise book. "We need to increase your speed for that 10k race."

"I'll be there."

"Good lad." He nods. "Everything OK?"

I shrug. "Yeah."

"Were those two idiots bothering you?"

"Just messing about."

"Sam," he smiles, "maybe long distance running isn't as 'cool' as football, but those lads will never have your stamina. It's OK to be different, you know. I had long hair back in the day, too. I was a real rocker." He shakes his short hair as if he's head-banging. I laugh for the first time all day.

"Get along now, or you'll be late."

On my way to English, I think about Mason and Pranav's insults. I'm not gay, but even if I was, it's none of their business.

I was going to tell Mum what's going on, and how I feel, but I can't seem to get the words straight in my head. I don't want to worry her. She works hard to make sure I can do athletics club, have decent trainers and kit.

When she's not working, she's always tired. Sometimes she sits in front of the TV and it doesn't even look like she's watching it. I've heard her crying at night, when she thinks I'm asleep.

I need to look after her. I can't let her down. I'm the man of the house now that Dad has left.

I have to step up.

CHAPTER 2

BREAKING POINT

Mum

Getting offered an extra shift tonight means Sam and I won't be going to the cinema for our usual Friday treat. Hopefully we can still go next week.

I plonk the laundry basket down on Sam's bed and push his laptop to one side. I'm tempted to open it to see if I can find out what he's so obsessed with lately, but no. That's how trust gets broken.

Sam's dad, Richard, has let Sam down twice in a row now by cancelling plans at the last minute. I've avoided calling him until now, but I can't let this go on much longer. He might know what's bothering Sam. Maybe they've had a man-to-man chat, or even a row, and Sam just hasn't told me. Sam's probably worried about girls or his athletics trials, or exams.

I sit on the edge of Sam's bed and call Richard.

"Hello?" A woman's voice.

I cough. "Um, sorry, can I speak to Richard?"

His new wife sighs loudly. "Janet?"

"Yes."

"RICHARD!" she yells, and then the line goes quiet. Has she hung up? How dare—

"What?" Richard says gruffly.

"When did you last speak to Sam?"

"Why?" After a long pause he grunts, "Might have missed a few calls."

Typical! My hand tightens around the phone. "A few visits, too. Richard, you need to keep in contact! He's your son. I understand you might have moved on, but it doesn't mean Sam has."

I don't care that Richard isn't my husband anymore, but he'll always be Sam's father. I wish he would step up to his responsibilities.

"Is this going to take long? I have an important meeting to get to."

I count to five. Can't make ten. "What the hell is more important than your son?"

"Stop screaming at me!"

"I'm sorry." I take a deep breath. "I'm worried about Sam. He hasn't been himself lately. He isn't eating much, staying up late, always on the laptop."

"That's nothing new," Richard chuckles. "He's always loved computer games."

Richard never did listen. "You always liked them more than he did! What if he's looking up dodgy stuff? There could be some creep trying to meet up with him. Or what if he's being bullied? Richard, what if he's the bully?"

"Why do you always think the worst?"

"I do not!"

"Yes, you do. Accused me of having an affair," Richard says.

"Well... you were!" I snap.

"Look. He's a teenage boy. He's curious. You knew this day would come, Janet. He's not going to stay your baby forever. He has his own life. Maybe he's chatting to his mates or has a crush on a girl. Give him some space."

"No. I don't WANT to give him space, Richard! That's what you like to do. Sam and I used to talk. He always told me everything and now it's

like I don't know him anymore. Speak to him.
Be his dad, like you're supposed to be!"

The phone hangs up from his end.

CHAPTER 3

HOME ALONE

Sam

"Mum!" I call through the letterbox. Silence. I heave my bags over my shoulder, search my pockets for the key and open the front door.

After the day I've had, it would be nice to see Mum's smile, and not just a cold, empty hallway.

My eyes flick to the coat rack. Empty, except for Dad's old raincoat. *I bet his new wife bought him a better one. He doesn't need his old raincoat anymore, just like he doesn't need his old family*. I try to shake the thought off.

A year ago, Dad asked Mum for a divorce.

Our life is better in some ways and worse in others. At least there aren't late-night screaming matches now. But I miss Dad's stupid jokes and our gaming marathons at the weekends. I miss him talking about Liverpool FC, even though I hate football.

Athletics is more my thing. Running. I'm training to get into the regionals this year, but it's hard to focus with the name-calling this term.

I find a note from Mum on the kitchen table.

Got another shift, love. There's chicken in the fridge. Please feed Snowball. Don't forget your homework! DO NOT be on that laptop all night!

I can't believe she's working. Again. We never have any time together these days. What about the cinema tonight? And I need to talk to her about stuff. Important stuff. Stuff that, right now, I feel brave enough to tell her, thanks to my online mates. But who knows how long I'll feel brave?

I get on well with Mum, always have. She had me when she was older and when I'm having a difficult day she tells me how she tried for years to get pregnant, so when I came along she was thrilled. Today, I could really do with hearing how precious and special I am.

I won't be able to talk to her tonight because, by the time she gets in, I'll be in bed. And she gets up early for her morning cleaning job.

Snowball, our fat cat, pads into the kitchen and starts rubbing up against my legs.

"Alright. Keep your fur on!"

Snowball gobbles down her cat food. I'm not hungry though. All the stress at school is making me lose my appetite.

How do I tell Mum what's going on? What if she thinks there's something wrong with me?

This is different from a few years ago when Dad

was depressed and spoke to a special doctor. I'm not sure anything can 'fix' me. Wonder what Dad would say if I told him? Would he think I was a freak too?

I throw open my bedroom door. Mum only comes in to put clean laundry on my bed, or if I'm here. She respects my privacy; I can trust her. Dad never used to knock. Mum sometimes jokes how tidy it is, but I like things in order. Especially when the rest of my life feels like such a mess.

Dumping my bags on the bed, I turn on my laptop. It's the first thing I do when I get in. All my tension fades, knowing that soon I'll be chatting to Taylor, Jamie and Skye. But my laptop is old so, while I wait, I grab my phone and dial Dad's number. Need to check if he's coming to parents' evening next week.

My laptop makes a loud whirring noise.

Since Dad left, I've seen him less and less. He cancelled our last two meet-ups.

No answer. Just a stupid voice asking me to leave a message. I hang up and start pacing around my room.

Mum said Dad gets bored easily, so maybe he got bored with us. He has new step-kids now. Twin girls aged five, Tilly and Milly, and a new wife. How long will they hold his interest? But he still has me, he shouldn't forget. Why can't there be room for all of us?

A creeping rage flushes up my neck as I stab at the screen on my phone again. This time, when it goes to voicemail, I say, "It's Sam. Remember who that is?" and then I end the call, throwing my phone across the room onto my bed.

If my message makes him sad or angry, I don't care. I hope it makes him feel something. I'm sad a lot these days. If he bothered to call or visit, then he'd know that.

I kick the door shut. I don't want to do maths homework. Can't be bothered with history or biology either. Usually, I don't mind those.

I log onto the forum, itching to talk to my real friends, even though we've never met. We make a good team: Taylor is the funny one, Jamie is the brave one and Skye is the sensible one. They don't make fun of me for having long hair, or for having all the questions I do. They accept me inside and out.

They understand who I really am. Why can't everyone else? No one has any idea what it's like being me.

CHAPTER 4

A LONG DAY

Mum

I bend down to pick up the local newspaper off the doormat and frown at the headline: *Online teen bullying on the rise.* Not what I want to think about after a twelve-hour shift.

Sam has been so quiet lately. Is that what he's going through? Is he getting bullied? He's tall and skinny, not an ounce of fat or muscle on him. And he wears his hair long, but so what?

The kitchen is quiet and clean. No dirty dishes. He's a good boy, so tidy. I hang up my coat and stroke Snowball.

It's midnight so I don't yell up the stairs in case Sam is asleep. Instead, I knock on his door softly and then open it.

He scrabbles to close his laptop.

He's glued to that machine these days. What's he looking at? What does he do on there?

"Hi Mum," he says. "Good shift?"

"It was OK. Did you eat?" I ask.

"Wasn't hungry."

His eyes keep drifting towards his laptop. I say sharply, "You've done all your homework then? Exams are coming up. Hope you're prepared."

"Umm…" Sam trails off, looking guilty.

He hasn't done it. He thinks I'm clueless because I work so much, but I know something is wrong. I thought it was the divorce, but now I'm not sure. I want him to talk to me when he's ready.

I don't want to push him, but if he won't open up...

"So you've just been playing those stupid computer games all night again?"

"No!" Sam says, looking up at me. "Anyway, computer games aren't stupid!"

"Yes, they are. A total waste of time. That's what your Dad used to do. A complete evening, gone!"

Sam fiddles with the corner of his pillowcase. "Some of them are great. They can teach you stuff."

I fold my arms. "So can your textbooks."

"It's just another way of learning, Mum. Different from when you were at school."

"So, what's going on at school? You haven't mentioned Pranav for ages. He hasn't been round since Dad left."

He shrugs. "Don't really see him anymore. People get into different things. We don't have any lessons together."

"Has he got a girlfriend?" I whisper this, in case he's embarrassed.

"What?"

"It will happen for you, love. Just be patient."

"Mum! I don't care about that!"

"What's bothering you then? And don't say 'nothing'."

He doesn't even look at me.

I sigh loudly. "Look, Sam, I know you feel like you know those people," I point to his laptop, "but you don't. You haven't met them in real life, so how can you talk to them? You need to be careful these days."

Sam rolls his eyes. "We've had internet safety

talks at school. I'm not stupid!"

"I know you're not stupid. It's more about who's on the other side of that screen, and their motivations. There's all this trolling now, and people hurting kids. People can say anything and pretend to be anyone."

"But Mum, sometimes it's easier to be honest online; to tell people things that are hard to say." Sam looks at me, biting his lip. His big brown eyes are sad. "I am careful, Mum. I talk to these friends every day. Have done for a year. And we've spoken on video chat so I know they are who they say they are. The only trolls I know are at school and they don't bother to hide behind a computer." He swallows.

"Oh, love. Are you being teased about having long hair again?" Sam's hair touches his shoulders and is very thick.

He squirms away from my outstretched hand. "They don't care if footballers have long hair.

It might be different if I was one of the footy lot, but I'm not. I can't even wear it down anymore. It's always tied back, and I still get called names."

"They are just jealous that they can't pull off the longhaired look!" I joke, trying to make him smile, but he looks like he might cry.

When he was a baby he was so happy all the time. Nothing bothered him for long. We called him Sunny Sam. But he hasn't been sunny for ages.

I hate working all the time. We don't see much of each other these days but, even though me working long hours is a big change, Sam needs to see that we can survive as a one-parent family.

He shakes his head and sounds angry. "You just don't get it, Mum. You wouldn't understand."

I put my hand on his arm. "I know it's difficult with Dad not around. I'm sorry. I'm doing my best. But you have to help me out! I can't work two jobs, come home and then nag you about your homework."

"Fine. Whatever. Stop going on," he grumbles, turning back to his computer.

"Samuel! You need to take some responsibility. If you start falling behind and your grades go down, then I'll have to take your laptop away."

"No! You can't do that!"

"I can and I will. Focus on your schoolwork."

CHAPTER 5

Sam

When I run, and I'm in the zone, I can forget everything. I focus only on the slap of my trainers on the tarmac. The rush of my heartbeat in my ears. I like being able to push myself. Seeing how far this body can go. I just wish it was a different body, that's all.

Looking one way, but feeling another, is like a battle in my head and body all the time.

For a few years, I've wondered if I will 'grow out of it', and change my mind about how I'm feeling, but I don't think I will. It's like someone telling me I'm not hungry when I know I'm starving.

As soon as I get in the front door, out of breath and sweaty, Mum is there, hanging up her coat.

I slip off my trainers.

She gives me a smile and opens her arms for a hug. "Sorry about last night," she says. She gives me a big squeeze and I hug her back, tightly.

"Look, your Dad finally rang. Says he'll be at parents' evening and then we'll all have dinner afterwards. Sound OK?"

"Yeah."

"You do know you can talk to me about anything, right? I was just really tired last night."

"Mum?"

"Yes?"

"I haven't really got any mates at school." Snowball purrs around my feet. "Can I talk to you about something?"

A sad smile covers her face. "Of course! I was hoping you would tell me what's bothering you."

But now that I've said that… I don't know where to start. Am I ready? I wish Taylor, or Jamie, or Skye could do this for me instead. How far back do I go?

"Have you heard of… GIDS?"

"Sam!" Mum puts her hand over her mouth. Her eyes narrow. "I thought Dad talked to you about protection and stuff! Have you caught something?"

Ewww. "Wha—? No! No. It's… I don't feel quite right. I feel like things aren't right."

"Oh, my god." Mum's lip starts wobbling. She's going to cry. "Is it drugs?"

"No! It's nothing like that."

This is harder than I thought. But now that I've

started I might as well go the whole way.

"It's—" I take a deep breath and remember what Jamie told me online. I can do this, be brave.

Mum loves me, no matter what.

"Mum," I stare right into her eyes. "I would really like it if you started calling me Samantha."

She almost laughs, but then frowns a tiny bit. "Sorry, what?"

"You always ask what I'm doing on my laptop? Well, come upstairs and I'll show you. I think I might be transgender."

CHAPTER 6
OUT IN THE OPEN

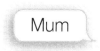

Sam and I sit on his bed with the laptop between us. He's just shown me the conversation between him and his online friends last night.

Taylor: *You've got this, Sammy. You know we love you.*

Jamie: *Telling my parents was the best thing I ever did. You'll be fine. And if they freak out, we're here.*

Skye: *Think of all the make-up you'll be able to share! No, seriously — if you tell her, maybe you can come to one of the Meet-Ups and we can actually hang out IN PERSON! Wouldn't that be great?*

They obviously care about Sam a great deal.

Tears prick my eyes, thinking of him up here, night after night, feeling like these were the only friends he could talk to. And there was me, crying over soap operas and wondering if I should have stayed with Richard for Sam's sake.

As I scroll through the different forums, Sam bites his nails, watching me. I'm silent, thinking and clicking on different pages. This is a lot to take in. I haven't heard of this before. Gay is one thing, but transgender? What does that mean for us, as a family?

I click onto the Parents' Support page. So much information! Will Sam need an operation? Do we have to legally change his name? Should he take hormones? What if he changes his mind?

But hold on. I can read this all later. Right now, he needs his mum.

"So, is the teasing about your hair a part of it?"

Sam shakes his head. "They think I'm gay."

"And you're not?"

"No, Mum. Being trans isn't the same as being gay. Gay is about who you fancy, but trans is about who you are. On the inside."

I nudge him with my elbow. "Wow! You've got this all figured out already, haven't you?"

He gives me the first real smile I've seen from him in months. "I have. That GIDS I asked you about? It's the Gender Identity Development Service. A special place for people thinking about this stuff."

"They can help?" I ask.

"Definitely. But their waiting list is over a year long."

"Oh. Seems like I've got some research of my own to do then. Can I borrow your laptop?" I say, looking down at the screen again.

Sam grins.

"Well, for now, maybe you could just book us an appointment with Dr Stewart. Maybe we could go together? He'll know who else can help," he says.

I smile at him. Girl, boy — what does it really matter? This baby grew inside me for eight months, before popping out early because he was so keen to discover the world. It's my turn to go on a journey with him, now. He'll still need all my love and care, just the same as always.

Sam flashes his — her! — beautiful smile at me. There are tears in her eyes as she whispers, "But Mum, who'll be the man of the house now?"

"Who needs men?" I laugh. "We'll be two women of the house instead!"

We hug, and I squeeze her extra tight. "You did often say that you didn't feel right, when you were tiny. That you felt 'funny'."

"Did I?"

I push the hair off her forehead. "Yes. From when you were about six. You went through a phase of dressing up in my clothes. Dad and I didn't think anything of it at the time, because lots of children do that. I'm glad you've talked to me about this. You've been sad for ages. I thought it was the divorce."

"Do you think Dad will go crazy?" Sam asks.

I squeeze her hands. "The idea might take a while for him to get his head around. But we're meeting for parents' evening, so we can talk more then."

"You could tell him about the forum maybe?"

"I could. It's great you've got friends who understand it Sam, but you'll need your family, too. I'll see if there's a local support group we can go to. Your schoolwork is important right now as well. So, maybe just a little less time on the laptop? At least until the athletics trials and exams are over."

He — she — nods. "OK."

I wonder how long she's felt this way. She never liked cars, or football — but then lots of boys don't, do they? That doesn't mean much.

My boy. Now, my girl.

But always, my Sunny Sam.

ABOUT THE AUTHOR

Emma Norry completed an MA in Screenwriting at Bournemouth University and a BA in Film. She has been writing and publishing short fiction in local writing competitions and magazines for over fifteen years.

She loves going to the cinema, reading books and playing video games with her two kids.

Thanks to Alex and Beth at Inclusive Minds (a brilliant team of consultants championing inclusion and diversity) for introducing us to Robin Craig through their Young Ambassadors for Inclusion project.

We consulted Robin on the sensitive subject matter in this story, to ensure that it was both authentic and responsible. We are very pleased with the result, and hope you are too.

Robin Craig is a PhD candidate at Roehampton University and Shakespeare's Globe, working on transgender and disabled performance in the 21st century. His research is funded by the Arts and Humanities Research Council and he has presented his work at Queen's University Belfast, King's College London and Roehampton University.